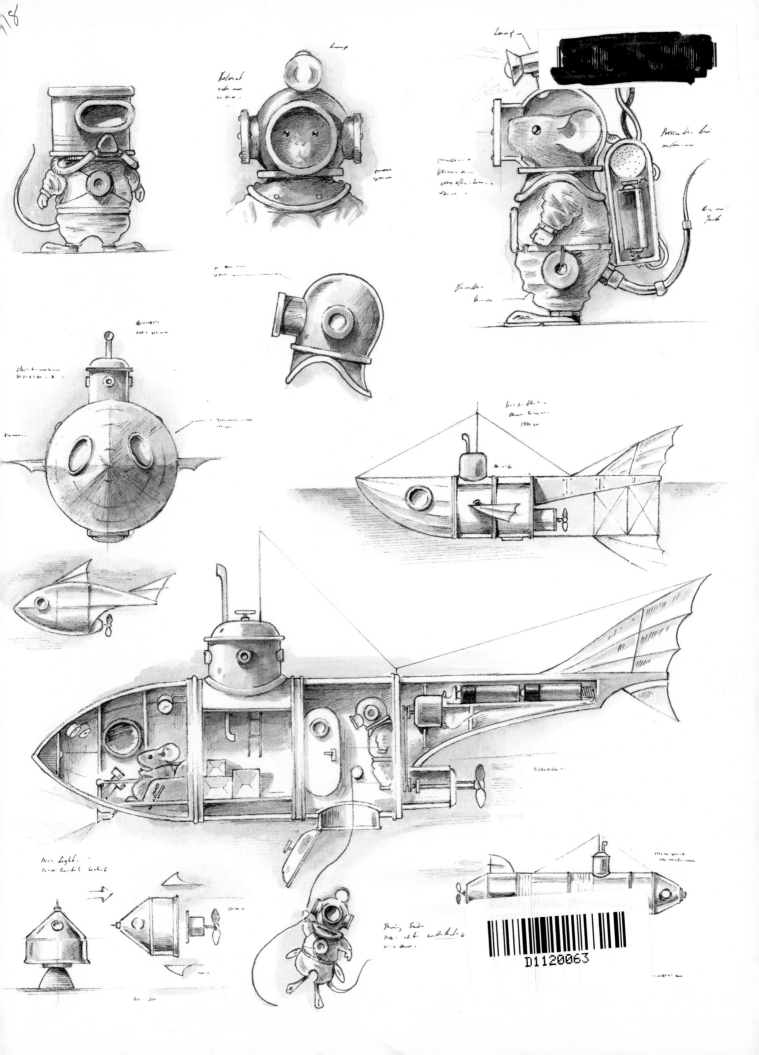

Fig 1

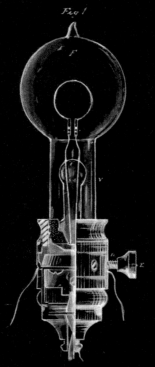

Attest
H H Howard
James A Byrn

Inventor
T. A. Edison
Dyer T W. Wilson
his Atty

EDISON

FSC
www.fsc.org
MIX
Paper from
responsible sources
FSC® C002795

Torben Kuhlmann

E D I S O N

The Mystery of the Missing Mouse Treasure

Translated by David Henry Wilson

North
South

1. The University of Mice

Ka-ching! The sound of the cash register rang through the bookstore.

"Let's go!" a mouse whistled, standing on a pile of books. Countless little mouse heads peeked out of their hiding places.

A small boy who was buying a comic book was so deep in conversation with the shopkeeper that neither of them was paying attention to what was happening around them. It was the perfect moment! One after another, the mice hopped out from behind the books and shelves, zipping across the room on silent feet before disappearing into a mouse hole in the far corner of the shop. After a short climb through the walls, the mice finally reached their destination.

Behind the shelves lay the University of Mice. Here any inquisitive mouse could learn everything there was to know about the history of mice: mice who had traveled the world, mice who had made great discoveries, and also the achievements of people. For example, the invention of the steam engine and the electric light.

The lectures were given by an elderly, gray-furred mouse professor whose white whiskers formed a rather messy mustache all around his nose. After a long day of lessons, he would go back to his study and enjoy a quiet evening in his armchair. His thoughts would wander back to the good old days. When he was young, the Professor had had many adventures on his great quest for knowledge. Now times were more peaceful, but unfortunately, in his view, they were also a bit more boring.

2. An Unfamiliar Face

Today there was someone in the lecture room whom the Professor had never seen before. A tiny pointed nose was poking out from behind the last row of chairs. The young mouse waited patiently until the lecture ended and all the mice made their way home. Then very timidly he went up to the front desk.

"Excuse me, Professor, but I need your help . . . ," he said shyly. "You see, I'm looking for a treasure."

The Professor listened attentively.

"Many years ago, my great-great-great . . ." The young mouse paused and started counting on his toes the number of *great*s it must have been. But then he decided it didn't really matter how many there were, and so he began again.

"Many years ago, one of my ancestors sailed across the Atlantic. And he took a large treasure with him."

"Aha!" said the Professor. "Where exactly did you get this information?"

"Here!" squeaked the little mouse, reaching into his pocket and pulling out a piece of paper, which he gave to the Professor. He was prepared for questions.

"He left this letter behind. He talks about the treasure and his journey to America. This piece of paper has been in our family's possession for generations. It's the last sign of life that we have of my ancestor."

The letter didn't look like an ordinary piece of paper. It was all crumpled and yellowed. It must have been very old. One edge was jagged, as if it might have been torn out of a book. The Professor studied the text. Written in old-fashioned mouse language, it did indeed tell the story of a sea voyage and a treasure.

"Please, Professor, help me find the treasure!" pleaded the young mouse.

At first the Professor didn't know what to say. After all, he was a mouse of great learning and didn't have time for such fantasies. Nevertheless, there was something about the little mouse's story that fascinated him.

"To tell you the truth," he said, "I'm not interested in missing treasures or maps with an X that marks the spot. But maybe we can find out more about your lost ancestor."

The young mouse beamed.

"Thank you, Professor!"

"What's your name?" the older mouse asked.

"Pete!"

3. Looking for Clues

The two mice rummaged through a drawer full of files and old documents. All they knew was that Pete's ancestor had sailed to America. The documents listed every ship that had ever crossed the Atlantic, and the only clue they had was the date on Pete's piece of paper.

"Look at this!" The Professor called Pete over. In one of the files was a photo that showed a group of people about to set sail on a ship to America. "Look closely," said the Professor. "There, among all the suitcases . . ."

The light was bad, and with the naked eye all they could see was a vague shadow. But they wanted to have a closer look, and so with a great effort the two of them heaved the heavy file out of the drawer and dragged it to a lamp.

The magnifying glass showed a mouse. It was Pete's ancestor! He was standing among the suitcases, posing proudly for the camera. The mouse actually looked a bit like Pete. But he had twisted his whiskers into a rather ridiculous handlebar mustache.

"Your ancestor must have liked having his photo taken with humans," said the Professor, who obviously found it a bit bold for a mouse to push his way into a people picture.

"We've found him!" squealed Pete in delight. The mystery was solved, and the treasure seemed close enough to touch. Only when and where did the ship arrive? That was the question. The Professor continued his search through the files and documents. . . .

The New-York Daily Time

VOL. L. NO. 15   NEW YORK, THURSDAY, SEPTEMBER 19, 1841   PRICE

TRANSATLANTIC LINER SINKS!

HMS »ATLANTIS« LOST DURING ATLANTIK CROSSING. LEAVING SEA-FIRE ON BOARD · NO CASUALTIES AMONG PASSENGERS

N.º OF SHARES

...LAND SHIPPING COMPANY Lᵗᵈ
Registered Office
...AST 22 H EXCHANGE BUILDINGS LIVERPOOL.

4. At the Bottom of the Sea

Oh dear! The ship the two mice were searching for had an accident and sunk many years ago. It had never reached America.

The Professor put on a pair of small round spectacles and began to read.

"It looks like all the passengers were saved," he said. But the article only reported on what happened to the humans. Not a word was mentioned about the fate of the mice who had been on board. No other trace of Pete's ancestor could be found, no matter how closely they looked through the magnifying glass. They looked through photos that were taken later of the ship's crew and all the rescued passengers, but there was no sign of the missing mouse.

Ships Lost On The Atlantic Ocean

5. The Treasure Map

With the help of the old newspaper clippings and entries from the ship's logbook, Pete and the Professor were able to piece together the events that had led up to the disaster. They marked the location of each one on a large map of the ocean. Where the line of the ship's progress ended, Pete drew a large X. This was the last known position of the liner. And so that must be where the mysterious treasure would be, at the bottom of the sea.

"Interesting," murmured the Professor. "What we have now really is a treasure map. And an X marks the spot. . . ."

The two mice studied the results of their investigation.

"That means the treasure will be lost forever," said Pete with a sigh. "Whatever my ancestor had with him will stay at the bottom of the sea for the rest of time. No mouse could ever get to it. Never!" He hung his head sadly.

The Professor looked into the distance and muttered meaningfully: "Hmmm, once upon a time there were similar things said about a mouse getting to the moon. . . ."

According to the Professor, nothing was impossible for a mouse. Pete listened eagerly to his stories. The Professor told him how once a mouse had learned to fly and had crossed the Atlantic in a wobbly plane. Many years later, the very first earthling to reach the moon had been a mouse.

"You see, one should never underestimate us mice," he said, finishing his lecture. "A mouse can also get to the bottom of the sea!"

"Incredible!" squeaked Pete, who was impressed but still not convinced. "Do you really think we could do it?"

"What do you mean 'we'?" asked the Professor with a sniff and a snort. "I'm far too old for such adventures. When you've grown up enough, you can go and look for the treasure yourself."

"But I thought we'd start preparing for our diving expedition right away!" said Pete, not giving up, but the Professor was not persuaded and finally started to leave.

"Delighted to have met you, Pete, and I wish you all the best."

"But Professor! . . ." Pete shouted again.

There was no reply.

6. Mice Underwater

The little mouse was on his own again. But Pete was determined not to give up. Hadn't the Professor told him about mice who had single-handedly learned to fly and even land on the moon?

"Very well then," he said to himself, "I'll find a way to land on the bottom of the sea."

Holding his breath and diving were not options. That would only give him a few seconds, as Pete had found out in the bathtub when he was a tiny mouse. He had to find a way to take the air with him. But how?

Pete began to scribble on a piece of paper. But his doodles still didn't bring him any ideas that might work. He looked around. On the table opposite him stood a glass of water.

"Air outside, water inside? Maybe I can just reverse the principle," he murmured. "Air in, and water out."

Pete tried different experiments to get small glasses to dive. But it wasn't easy to make the air go under the water. Even the smallest diving bells pushed their way up to the surface. He had to keep pushing them down again, or attaching a heavy weight to them. Ah, maybe that was the answer!

He would attach the glass to a weight and dive with it himself. To be on the safe side, he decided first to try it in the bathtub. If it worked, he would repeat the experiment in the harbor or in the sea.

The water level rose higher and higher, but apart from his wet feet, Pete generally stayed dry.

"It works!" he squeaked. His voice sounded quiet and muffled. The bell was now almost completely submerged. He was very excited— he had proved that he could design a real diving bell. In order to resurface, he pulled the thread that tied the weight to the bell.

SNAP! The thread broke off in Pete's hand. How would he get out now?

"Pete, what are you doing?!" shouted the Professor, jumping into the tub to save him.

"I came back because I had a feeling you wouldn't give up. You're a stubborn little fellow, aren't you?" The Professor wiped the water off his whiskers. Then he shook himself from head to toe like a wet dog.

"Well, I can't say I'm surprised. I was the same in the old days. When I was young, I also went off on crazy adventures, risking life and limb like an idiot. Anyway, the first thing we need to do now is get out of here before the owner comes home."

"Thank you," said Pete, his voice trembling. "Thank you for saving my life!"

Soon afterward, the two mice were standing in the somewhat untidy home of the Professor. It looked almost like a small museum. The shelves were bursting with objects, books, and scraps of paper; and there were photos and newspapers hanging on the walls.

"Who are they?" asked Pete, looking at all the pictures.

"Some of the most important inventors in the history of the world . . . and my heroes!"

Pete nodded his head in admiration, while the Professor rummaged around in various boxes.

"So you really want to get that treasure from the bottom of the sea?" asked the Professor. "Very well . . ." He paused thoughtfully. "Then I'll help you."

Pete gazed at him wide-eyed. Had he heard right?

"I may not be as young as I was," said the Professor with a grin, "but I'm not ready for the scrap heap yet!"

In his hands was an old photo.

Pete gasped. "That was YOU who landed on the moon?"

The Professor nodded humbly and said, "And in spite of what some believe, the moon is, unfortunately, not made of cheese."

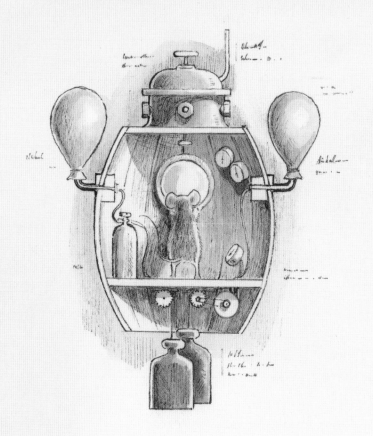

7. A New Attempt

"Your idea with the diving bell wasn't completely wrong," explained the Professor. He was drawing something on a piece of paper.

"We need a hatch and a few weights at the bottom . . . and balloons to resurface. And we'll take some air with us too. Compressed air. He mumbled to himself until the drawing was finished.

The two mice spent the next few days looking for the right components. Instead of a glass dome, the Professor suggested they use a wooden spice container. He said it was easier to work with wood.

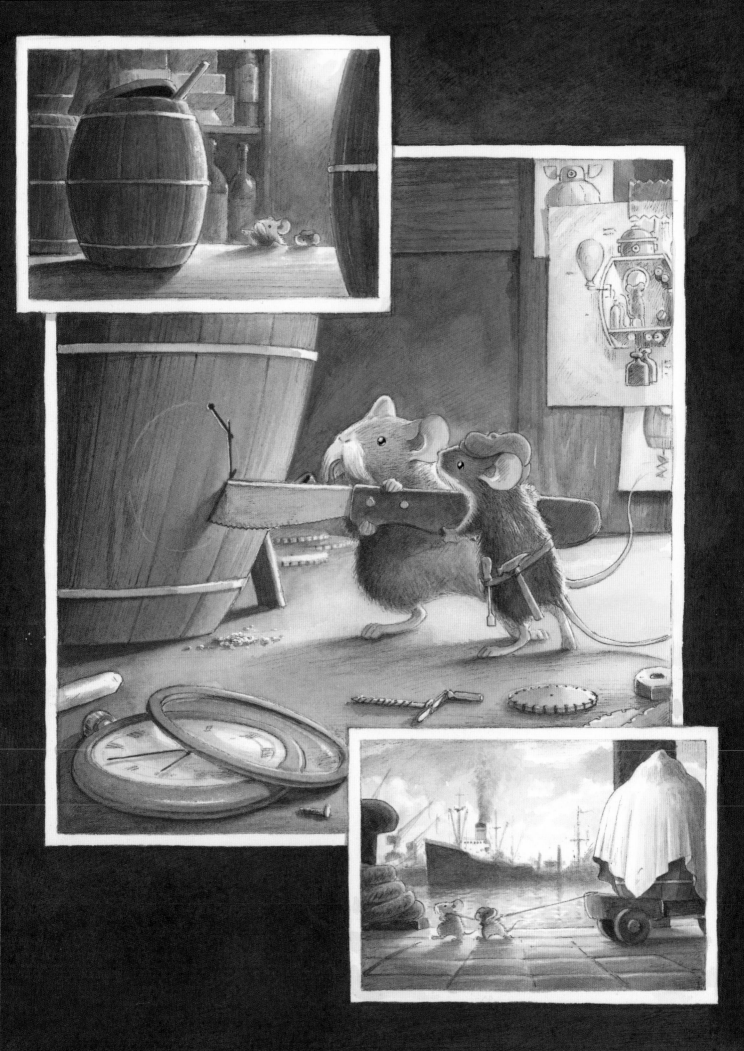

The Professor turned a valve to let the air out of the balloons, which were attached to the outside like water wings. The diving bell disappeared beneath the waves. Several weights now dragged the two mice, their invention, and the compressed air down into the depths.

"It works! We're diving!" cried Pete. "I can even see the bottom of the ocean!"

The weights settled on the seabed. A few crabs scuttled out of their hiding places to have a look at the two mice. The Professor didn't like the crabs being so close, so he quickly turned the valve in the other direction. The first balloon filled with air and started to carry the diving bell upward. But one of the crabs swung its sharp claw at the balloon. The balloon popped in a cloud of bubbles, and the second balloon burst too.

Pete and the Professor were trapped! Now what? Without the balloons they couldn't get back to the surface. There was only one hope: they would have to open the hatch and swim as fast as they could.

"Don't be afraid, Pete," said the Professor. "You can do it!" And so saying, he turned the handle of the little glass door. "Get ready. Take a deep breath. Go!"

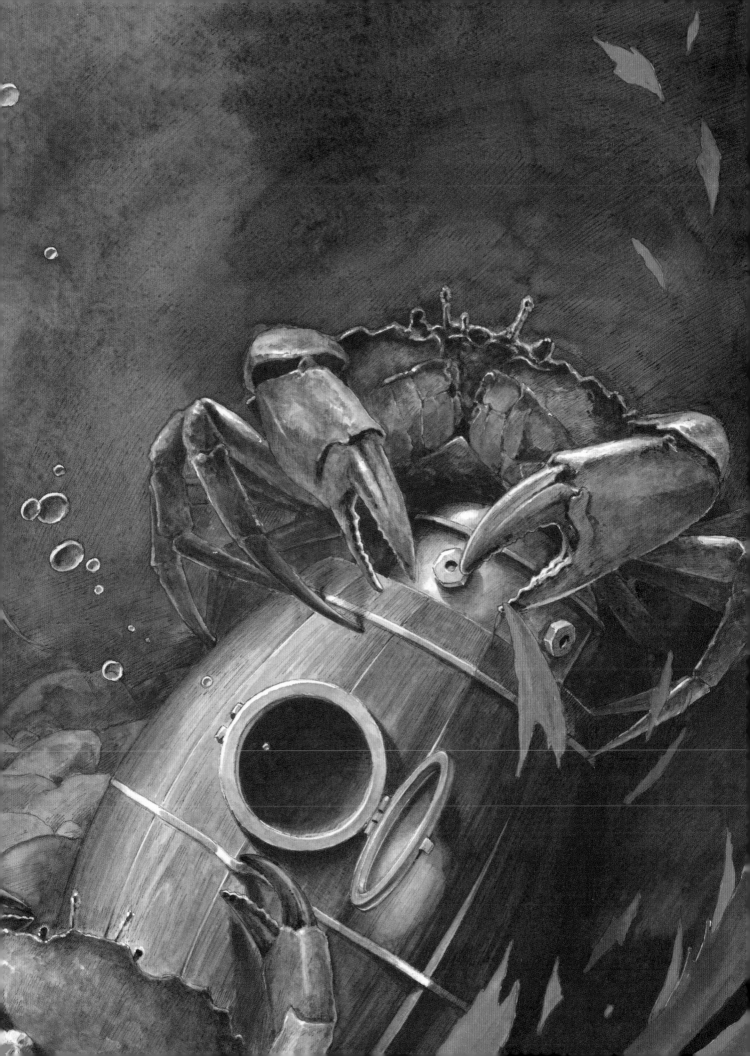

The two mice were agreed: a diving bell was not the best way to get to the bottom of the sea. In principle it worked, but in practice they needed something that would enable them to move around under the water. The question was: What? The Professor filled one piece of paper after another with his drawings, and one piece of paper after another ended up in a crumpled ball on the floor.

"It's no good," he said at last. "We need to approach the problem scientifically. . . ."

8. Nature Studies

Pete had never seen so many fish in all his life. Speechless, he pressed his nose against the cold glass of the huge fish tank.

"Nature has the answer to a lot of our problems," said the Professor. "There are thousands of creatures that live deep down in the ocean. So maybe we'll find the perfect solution here."

He unrolled the sheets of paper he had brought with him, lit a candle, and once again began to draw. This time, though, he didn't draw ideas for diving bells. He was studying the body structures of the fish that were gliding so elegantly with their fins and tails through the water in front of him.

The clever mice had a plan. They would build a submarine with a tail and fins just like a metallic fish!

On the way back, Pete looked around in wonderment. He saw more fish tanks, skeletons of small fish, and shelves full of snail and mussel shells. He wasn't even listening to the Professor, who was striding on ahead, talking to nobody about his ideas for the submarine. His voice got quieter and soon became nothing but an echoing whisper through the large rooms of the aquarium. Then suddenly, there was complete silence. Pete was alone. Around him was nothing but dark cupboards and glass tanks.

Octopus Model

Pete's heart was pounding wildly. He ran out of the room as fast as he could, and when he looked back he saw a sign above the door. In large letters it read:

The Terrors of the Deep.

Then someone tapped on his shoulder from behind, and he jumped and let out a shrill scream. Luckily it was only the Professor, who had come back to look for him.

"Are there really such monsters in the deep?" asked Pete, his voice still trembling with fear.

The Professor poked his nose into the room.

"Well, I wouldn't exactly call them monsters," he said. "But yes, there are some very strange creatures at the bottom of the sea."

"Hmm . . . well, maybe it would be better to . . . um . . . leave them in peace . . . ," said Pete.

"No need to be afraid," said the Professor soothingly, and he showed Pete the sketches he had been drawing. "Our submarine will be nice and solid. Nobody will be able to eat us up. And we do not have to be afraid of the biggest of the sea creatures anyway."

"The biggest ones?"

"Yes, in spite of their size, the only things they eat are little shrimp. Look over there!" He pointed upward to the blue whale skeleton hanging from the ceiling. "Our submarine will be too large for them to eat."

WHALES

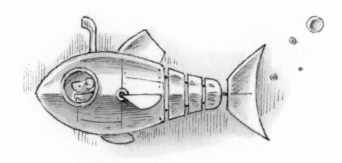

9. A Mouse Submarine

The list of tasks to complete was long. First, the Professor wrote down a series of numbers. Then he wrote down some symbols, crossed out the first numbers, and wrote down some new ones. Pete watched with interest.

"Do you remember how we had to escape from our diving bell and swim to the surface?"

Pete nodded.

"Did your ears hurt then?"

Pete nodded again.

"The deeper we go, the more pressure the water puts on us. Just imagine a tower of water hundreds of feet high, right above our heads. What we need is some thick, solid outer walls and some thick, solid diving suits."

The Professor drew two thick, solid lines under the results of his calculations.

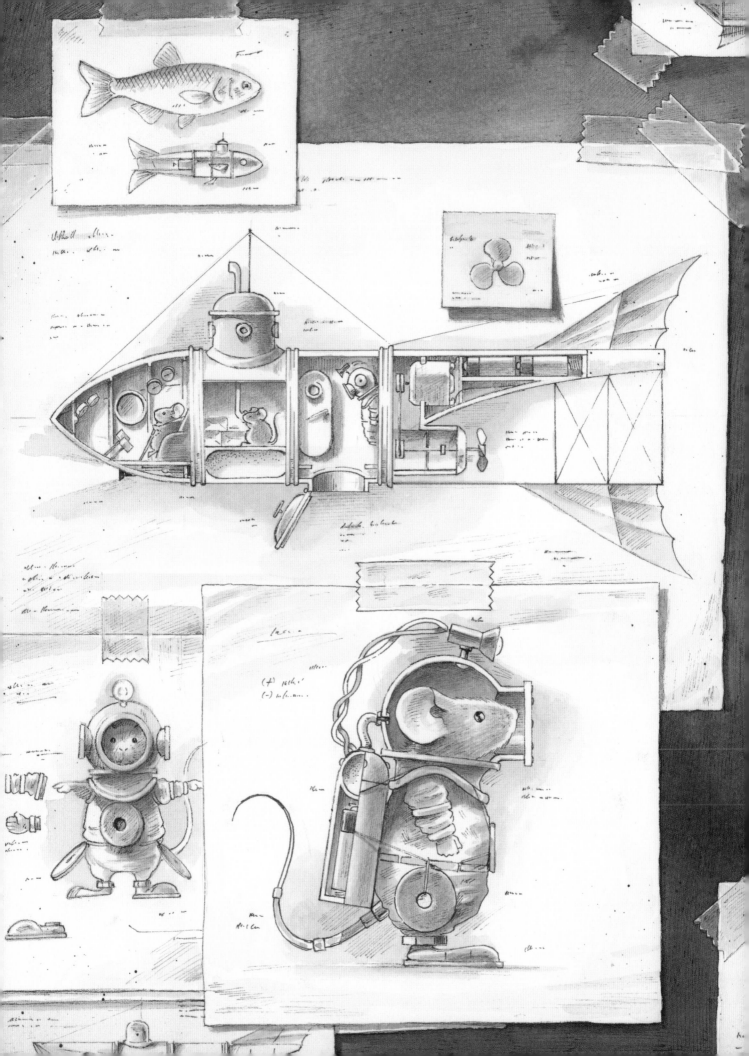

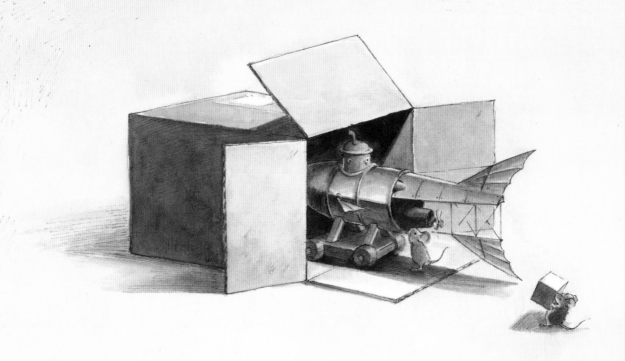

10. Getting Ready to Go

Finally, the submarine was ready. Pete and the Professor had worked on it night after night. It would have been too dangerous to do it in the day, because curious humans could easily have caught them. How would they have reacted if they'd seen two mice welding steel, molding the components, and then screwing everything together to create this magnificent invention?

Now the time had come to plan the journey. First, Pete and the Professor had to get to the spot where the ship carrying Pete's ancestor had sunk. According to the Professor, that was the least of their problems. He already had a plan. They would do the first stage of their journey as stowaways, hidden in a box on a cargo ship. As soon as they reached the right place, they would dive overboard in their submarine.

What a scare! Pete and the Professor didn't expect to see a cat on board. But as it turned out, the cat was not in the least bit interested in hunting mice. Over the years it had probably become accustomed to eating fish, potato soup, and other dishes that sailors eat, and so it had lost its appetite for not-so-tasty mice. At least that was the Professor's theory.

Very carefully the two mice dragged the submarine across the deck and past the portholes, through which they could hear the crew laughing and singing. Luckily no one saw them. The two mice stood at the front of the ship, in front of one of the holes through which the anchor ropes passed.

They closed the hatch and waited for the next big wave. It worked! The submarine slipped into the water. SPLASH!

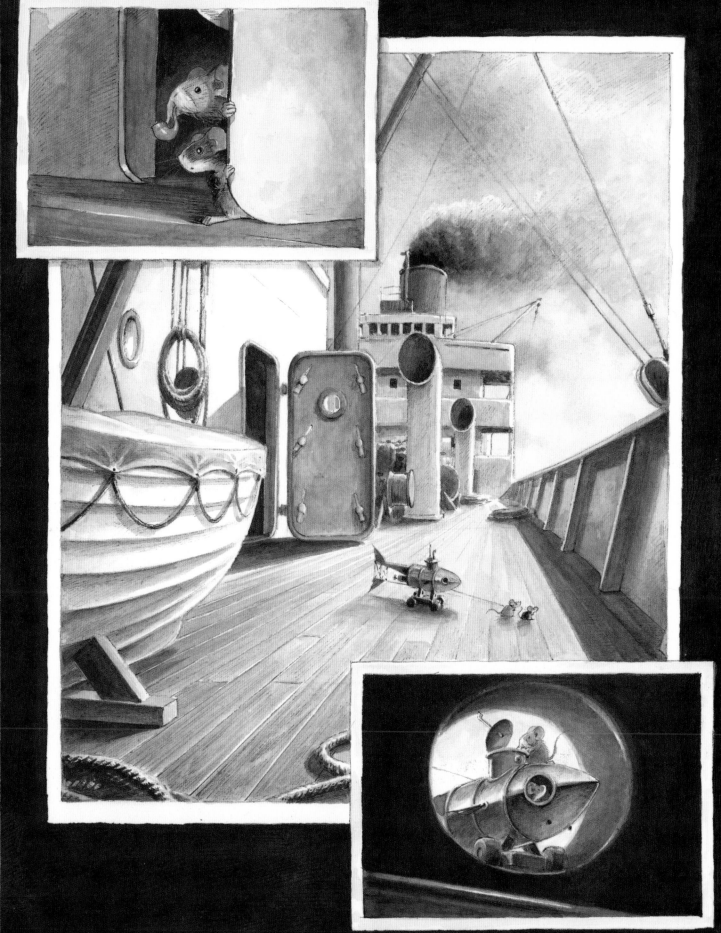

11. Down in the Depths

The submarine with the two excited adventurers on board slid down just below the surface of the water. The propeller started to hum. Pete kept a very close eye on the instrument panel. Water pressure. Air supply. All the indicators were green, and not a single drop of water had penetrated the outer shell. The Professor pushed the helm forward, sending clouds of bubbles whooshing out on either side. Pete flooded the air chambers so that the ship would be heavier. And they dived down into the depths of the ocean.

The two mice looked out through the thick glass windows. A school of fish swam around them a few times and then disappeared into the distance. The sunbeams that sparkled in the waves above soon vanished as well. A shadow fell over the submarine, and suddenly they heard a loud booming sound.

"What's that?" squeaked Pete, covering his ears. All the loose metal parts around them started to rattle.

"It's a whale singing!" cried the Professor.

Pete gazed wide-eyed and openmouthed at the giant animal.

"He must be a hundred times bigger than a mouse. . . ."

Still shaking their heads in amazement, the mice steered their ship under the monster and down into the depths. It was getting darker and darker, because the light couldn't reach so far down. At the same time, Pete's instrument panel showed that the water pressure was rising. The metal creaked and groaned under the stress, but the submarine held firm.

12. The Treasure

Little by little, the bow of a giant ship emerged in the darkness. The metal was all twisted and eaten away by rust. Pete and the Professor found the wreck! It was the exact spot at the bottom of the Atlantic where they had calculated it would be. But could they find Pete's ancestor's treasure? The Professor carefully steered the submarine through the rusty skeleton of the big ship. Soon the two mice were standing in the airlock, dressed in their heavy diving suits, ready to explore every inch of the wreck.

They spotted the ship's treasure! It gleamed in the light of their lamps. But that was not the treasure they were in search of. They continued on to the farthest corner of the ship, passing through endless dark corridors, until they came to what had once been the ship's kitchen. A few things were surprisingly well preserved: plates and dishes, and also bottles of wine and rum. Next to the kitchen was the pantry, and if a mouse had sailed on this ship, the food store would certainly have been his hiding place.

"Look over here!" cried Pete. It was a small trunk. Something had been carved into the metal front: the sign of a mouse. Pete had found his ancestor's treasure chest!

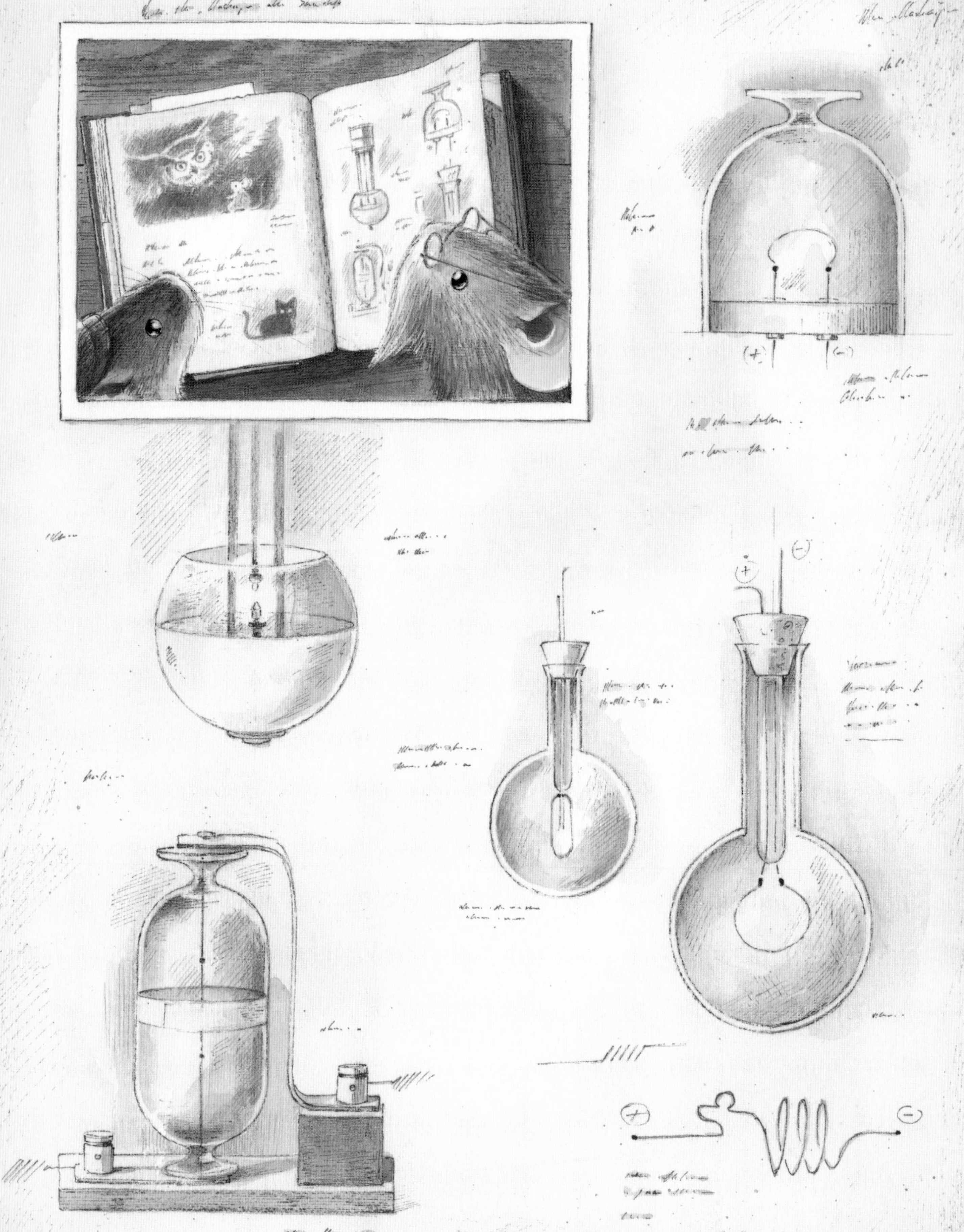

13. The Secret of the Mouse Treasure

The treasure that Pete's lost ancestor had taken with him to cross the Atlantic did not consist of gold coins, pearls, and jewels, as one might have expected. For years and years, what had been resting in this little chest at the bottom of the sea was a book. It was the diary of an inventor! With mounting astonishment, Pete and the Professor looked through the yellowed pages. The handwritten notes described hard times in the mouse world, with pitch-black mouse caves and predators lurking in the dark shadows. But they also found drawings and designs that were meant to make mouse life simpler and safer. Pete and the Professor found one of these inventions particularly fascinating. Right at the end of the little book were ideas for a special apparatus: a pear-shaped glass object with some wires inside. But where the final design should have been, there was nothing. The last two pages were missing. Someone had torn them out.

"Pete, show me your ancestor's letter again," said the Professor.

Pete rummaged in his bag. He pulled out the piece of paper that had started this whole adventure.

"Here it is!" He gave the paper to the Professor. "What are you thinking?"

"Just an idea . . ."

The page fit. The letter from Pete's ancestor was one of the two missing pages. The two mice read more of the now-almost-complete diary.

"But there's still a page missing," said Pete.

The Professor carefully looked through all the inventions, paying special attention to the strange glass object with wires inside. Then he looked at the photos on the wall.

"Eureka!" he cried, and went rushing out.

"What have you found?" asked Pete, hurrying after him. He could hardly keep up with the old mouse.

The Professor climbed up a bookcase, pushed some of the clothbound books to one side, and opened a thick encyclopedia.

"$A \ldots B \ldots C \ldots D \ldots E \ldots$," he murmured to himself.

"What are you doing, Professor?" asked Pete, who was now standing by the bookcase and had no idea why the Professor was getting so excited.

"Now I know what happened to your ancestor! And to his invention!"

THOMAS A. EDISON

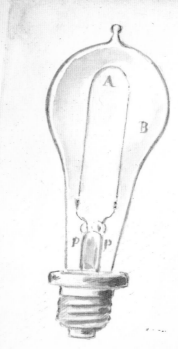

Edison's Light
Bulb

FIG. 15. — The principle of electric lighting

There he was! It was the same mouse with the funny handlebar mustache–Pete's long-lost ancestor. In this photo too he was posing proudly for the camera, although you needed a magnifying glass to see him. And so he had survived. He had not gone down with the ship and his treasure. This was proved by the date of the photo, which had been taken much later. The proud little mouse inventor was holding a piece of paper, and the edge was jagged. It had to be the page that was missing from the diary.

When he escaped from the sinking ship, he obviously couldn't take the whole of his treasure with him and so he had torn out the most important page. And when Pete and the Professor looked very, very closely, they could actually see what was on the page.

A lightbulb.

But no, not *a* lightbulb—it was the *very first* lightbulb.

"Who is the man in the picture?" asked Pete.

"He was a great human inventor," said the Professor. "Apparently his greatest invention was made with the help of a certain mouse. . . ."

Pete slowly spelled out the name that accompanied the photo:

Thomas A. Edison.

EDISON'S MOUSE
~ *The Inventor of the Light Bulb* ~

The End

The Historical Facts

The Invention of the Electric Light

For many people the name Thomas Alva Edison is mainly associated with the invention of the electric lightbulb, but it would be more accurate to say that he improved its efficiency and made it into a marketable product. Who really invented it remains controversial. It may not have been a mouse who got the first wire to glow, but during the nineteenth century there were many inventors and engineers who contributed to the development of the lightbulb.

In 1802 the English chemist **Sir Humphry Davy** succeeded in getting a platinum filament to glow. In 1809 he invented the carbon arc lamp, in which an electric current passed through two graphite electrodes and formed an arc of light between them.

Some people regard the Scottish inventor **James Bowman Lindsay** as the true inventor of the lightbulb. He demonstrated continual electric lighting in 1835.

The first patent was taken out in 1841 by the English inventor **Frederick de Moleyns,** who produced a light with powdered charcoal and fine platinum wires in an airless glass cylinder.

In 1860 the British physicist and chemist **Joseph Wilson Swan** constructed an electric lightbulb for everyday use, and he patented it in England in 1878—two years before Edison patented his own in the United States.

In Germany many people regard **Heinrich Göbel**, who emigrated to the United States, as the real inventor. He claimed to have produced light with carbon filaments in empty perfume bottles in 1854. However, he was unable to prove his case when the matter went to court.

Illustration 1: Sir Humphry Davy

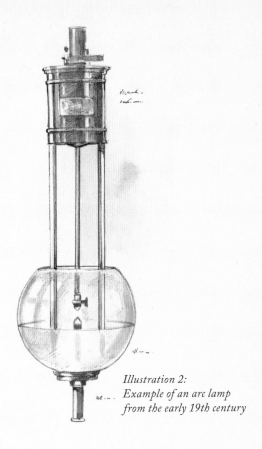

Illustration 2:
Example of an arc lamp
from the early 19th century

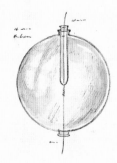

Illustration 3:
Design for a light bulb
by Frederick de Moleyns

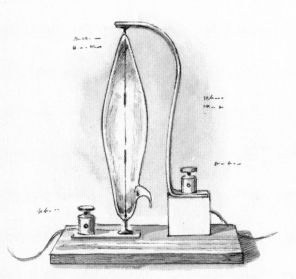

Illustration 4:
Experimental light bulb
by Joseph Wilson Swan

Illustration 5: Joseph Wilson Swan

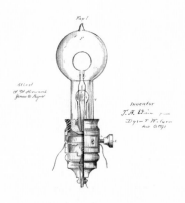

Thomas Alva Edison

Thomas A. Edison was one of the most important inventors and entrepreneurs who launched the age of electricity in the nineteenth century. Even as a young man he made his mark by improving existing techniques of telegraphy. The telegraph was a means of sending simple messages by passing electric signals through a wire. In the course of his life, Edison created numerous inventions, including the phonograph—an apparatus that could record sounds and replay them. Most people, however, think of him as the man who introduced electric lighting. In the midnineteenth century, existing methods of using electric currents to produce light were very unreliable and less suitable for daily use than the far more common gas lamp. This all changed with the lightbulb that Edison developed in 1879 and patented a year later. A carbon filament produced the light inside an airless glass container. These bulbs initially provided light for almost fifteen hours, but during the years that followed, Edison was able to prolong their life considerably. He was also the driving force behind the electrification of New York. Many other cities followed suit, and his companies expanded the networks and manufactured huge quantities of lightbulbs.

Thomas A. Edison (1847–1931) spent his entire life in the United States. He took out well over one thousand patents, but his name will forever be linked with the electric lightbulb. The screw form is still sometimes called the Edison screw base.

Illustration left:
Thomas A. Edison with lightbulb

The Author

Torben Kuhlmann was born in Sulingen, Germany, in 1982 and studied illustration and communications design at the Hochschule für Angewandte Wissenschaften, Hamburg. He finished his studies in 2012 with the picture book *Lindbergh—Die abenteuerliche Geschichte einer fliegenden Maus* [English title: *Lindbergh—The Tale of a Flying Mouse*], which was published soon afterward by NordSüd Verlag. It very quickly became a best seller and has now been translated into more than thirty languages. The picture book *Armstrong—Die abenteuerliche Reise einer Maus zum Mond* [English title: *Armstrong—The Adventurous Journey of a Mouse to the Moon*], published in 2016, tells the story of a mouse's first flight into space. In *Edison*, the third volume in this series about adventurous mice, the hero does not soar to hair-raising heights but dives to the deepest depths of the ocean.

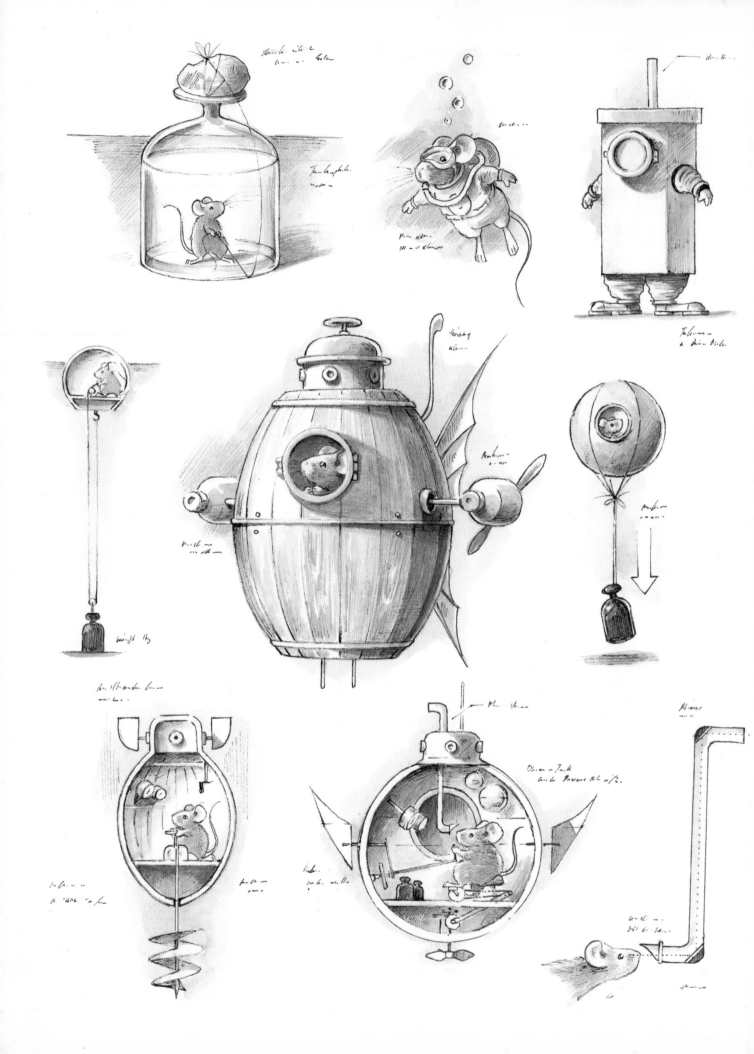